jE MCCANNA Tim
Bitty Bot's big beach getaway /
McCanna, Tim,

MAY 2 5 2018

WITHDRAWN

D0618227

T1-AVD-769

WITHDRAWN

BITTY BOT'S
BIG BEACH GETAWAY

WRITTEN BY **Tim McCanna**   ILLUSTRATED BY **Tad Carpenter**

A PAULA WISEMAN BOOK

Simon & Schuster Books for Young Readers · New York · London · Toronto · Sydney · New Delhi

For Sylvie Frank, who believed in Bitty Bot—T. M.

To my friend Jason "JJ" Jones—T. C.

SIMON & SCHUSTER BOOKS FOR YOUNG READERS · An imprint of Simon & Schuster Children's Publishing Division · 1230 Avenue of the Americas, New York, New York 10020 · Text copyright © 2018 by Tim McCanna · Illustrations copyright © 2018 by Tad Carpenter · All rights reserved, including the right of reproduction in whole or in part in any form. · SIMON & SCHUSTER BOOKS FOR YOUNG READERS is a trademark of Simon & Schuster, Inc. · For information about special discounts for bulk purchases, please contact Simon & Schuster Special Sales at 1-866-506-1949 or business@simonandschuster.com. · The Simon & Schuster Speakers Bureau can bring authors to your live event. For more information or to book an event, contact the Simon & Schuster Speakers Bureau at 1-866-248-3049 or visit our website at www.simonspeakers.com. · Book design by Jessica Handelman · The text for this book was set in Write Heavy. · The illustrations for this book were rendered digitally. · Manufactured in China · 0218 SCP · First Edition · 10 9 8 7 6 5 4 3 2 1 · CIP data for this book is available from the Library of Congress. · ISBN 978-1-4814-4931-1 · ISBN 978-1-4814-4932-8 (eBook)

At the beach in Botco Bay,
robots love to splash and play.

All except for Bitty Bot.
Fun vacation? Maybe not.

RUSTPROOF ROBOT OIL 4 SALE!

"Sun's too hot and sand's too gritty. Let's go back to Robot City."

Bitty's parents say, "Not yet. Haven't even gotten wet!"

"You need rustproof robot oil.
Cover every cog and coil."

Moments later, Bitty spots
two unhappy little bots
sitting sadly by the sea.
"Maybe they could play with me."

"What's the matter?
Why so blue?"

"We want something fun to do!"
Bitty gives the beach a scan.

"Come on, bots. I've got a plan."

"Time for us to mobilize!
First, we'll need a few supplies. . . ."

Bottles, barrels, bucket, bench,
hammer, pliers, socket wrench,
soda cans, a coil of rope,
drainpipe for a periscope.

Robots gather at the scene.
"Bots, behold our submarine!"

"Can we take it for a ride?"
"Absolutely! Jump inside!"

"My name's Clank and this is Smitty."
"You can call me Captain Bitty!"

Fish and coral. Crabs and snails.
Stingrays, turtles, sharks, and whales.

Giant squid! A sunken ship!
"Now we're talking. What a trip!"

As they travel
through the deep,
warning signals
flash and beep!

"Whoa! The sub has sprung a leak!"
Things are looking pretty bleak.

Sinking deeper. Down, down, down.
Crashing in a mermaid town!

Stranded on the ocean floor.
"How will we get back to shore?"

Captain Bitty calls for help.
Mermaids offer leafy kelp!

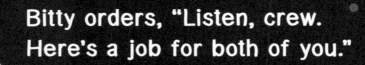

Bitty orders, "Listen, crew.
Here's a job for both of you."

"Ready? On the count of three, pop the hatch and follow me!"

Bots kick up a cloud of bubbles,
zooming from their deep-sea troubles!

Grateful to be back on land.
Good to see the sun and sand.

"Hope this beach trip never ends!
Mama, meet my new best friends!"

"Bitty Bot, it's time to go."
"What, already? No! No! No!
Five more minutes? Can't we stay?"
Papa Bot says, "Well, okay."

"Hurry! We can fix the sub!"
So they scramble, scrape, and scrub.

Add some parts and when they're done . . .
"Now it's made for everyone!"

Captain Bitty saves the day,
finding friends at Botco Bay.

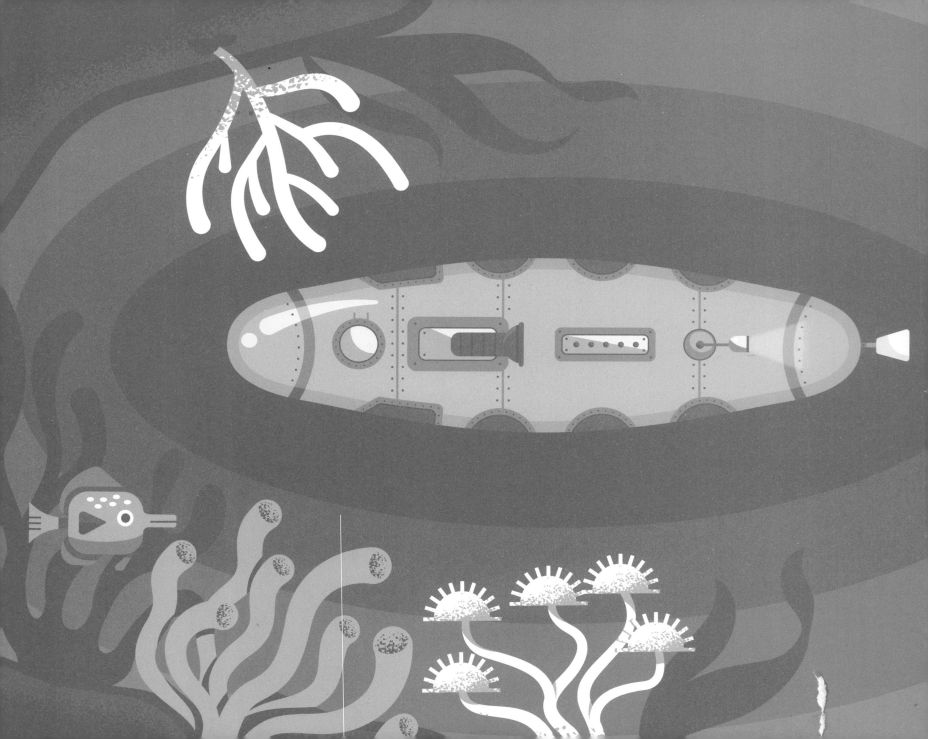